I, Trissy

I, TRISSY

Norma Fox Mazer

A YEARLING BOOK

Published by
Dell Publishing Co., Inc.
1 Dag Hammarskjold Plaza
New York, New York 10017

Yearling ® TM 913705, Dell Publishing Co., Inc.

ISBN: 0-440-44109-9

Reprinted by arrangement with Delacorte Press

Printed in the United States of America

One Previous Yearling Edition

New Yearling Edition
February 1986

10 9 8 7 6 5 4 3 2

CW

For my parents, Michael and Jean Fox

I, Trissy

DECLARATION OF INDEPENDENCE

When in the curse of human events, it becomes necessary for one people to dissolve the plitical bandds which have connected them with anothe%r, and to assume among the powers of the eart....to assume among the powers of the earth....

that's all I can remember power os the earth duh duh dumb dumb

When in the course of human events, it becomes necessary for one father to give his daughtera typewriter...she knows it's a bribe....

"Is this a bribe, Daddy?" I said.

"What do you mean by that, Trissy Jane?" It's always Trissy Jane when he's irritated, just Tris when he likes me.

"A bribe to keep my mouth shut," I said.

1

"Your mouth shut? Why would I want you to keep your mouth shut? Except for the obvious reason that you do put your foot in it an inordinate amount of the time. But what is there to keep your mouth shut about now?"

"You and Mom," I said. He just looked at me. "Besides, you never brought us presents before." When he was living home with us, I meant. Just since he's gone to live on his own, he brings things all the time. This typewriter is the biggest present I ever had. It must have cost plenty! It's not a little junky toy like I had last year.

The dumb thing is I loved this typewriter the minute I saw it. What Dad said when he gave it to me was, "Tris, now you can put down on paper all the things you're always making the mistake of saying out loud, and nobody has to know about them except you. It will probably

2

make life pleasanter for everyone."

I wanted to kiss him and say thank you
and all that, and instead I popped out with
that about the bribe.

"Do you want me to return it?" Dad said.

"No."

"You sure?"

"Yes." I said it again, louder. "YES,
I'M SURE!" But I was still thinking it was
a bribe.

Hello, Bribe, ~~MYXXXttiextypewxikexxpet~~
hello, my little tyepwriter pet. Don't get
your feelings hurt. I do like you. You're
a sweet little black thing with pretty silver
keys, and it's not your fault you're a bribe.

When Mother heard I'd said that about a
bribe (Blabbermouth Baby Boy Robert told)
she said that I oughtn't to look a gift horse
in the mouth. "Every little extra helps now,"

she said. "Though he might have been a lot more practical." You can always count on Mother to say something like that.

Also you can count on Mother to let me know that BBB Robert "takes things" better than I do, even if he is only six plus eleven/twelfths, while I am eleven plus six/twelfths.

She means about the separation. That's what she said the day Daddy moved out. I was over at Steffi's that afternoon, and when I got home, Dad was gone, and so was most of his stuff.

"We told you," Mother said. "We prepared you. Now don't you start getting sulky on me. You'll see your father almost as much as you ever did, I expect."

"Where is he? Why isn't he home?"

"Trissy! I'm going to scream if you ask that once more. Your father and I have explained this and explained this to you and

4

your brothers. You don't see Mitch or Robert

sulking, do you? Robert is young, but he takes

things one hundred percent better than you do."

   Mitch and Robert. Barf. Mitch takes

Mother's side on everything. And Robert is so

dumb he thinks it's FUN to see Daddy just on

Saturdays and go xxxxxx places with him. Dad

used to stick up for me, but now he's gone.

That's why I got the typewriter, I guess.

I, Trissy

HELLO, TYPEWRITER

HOW YOU DOING?

HOW YOU KEEP YOUR LETTERS GROOVING?

I love to tip and type on my tapwriter...I

love the sound it makes click click click clcik

click click click click click clock clickl clock

clidk click lick dlick click click click it

sounds so sleepy.....are you tired, Typewriter?

WAKE UP, STUPID!

What should I write?

I want to write something, but I don't

have anything special to write.

Mrs. Gilfer in English class says write

anything that comes into your head and pretty

soon you will be writing something that will

surprise you. What comes into my head? Nothing.

I'm dumb. I'm Steffi's best friend. I'm I'm

I'm Im Im.....bla blah blah....f is my favorite

letter...ffffffffffffffffffff cute little fff men

all in a row...also I like s, it's cozy and
sleepy sssssssssssss and snakey.....and o
is pretty cute itself ooooooooooo all little
o faces, little o mouths, and little o eyes
so scared and small looking o, o, o, oh, oh,
oh! oh dear!
Oh dear, nighttime is near
Trissy my love you are so queer

My Gang!
I love me
And me loves me
And together the three of us
Play happily.

Trissy, Trissy, don't be late
Mom's in the kitchen till half past eight
Little brother Robert licked your spoon
Big brother Mitch hit him with a broom

And poor Daddy won't be home tonight

Cause he can't stand the way we fight.

And now a station break, folks, with a few words

from our sponsor:

Are you hungry, thin, and undernourished? Try

NOURISHING NUTRITIOUS TRISS GERM today. It's

Chewy, Crunchy, and Crispy. It's full of nuts.

Sprinkle some on your cream of wheat. Mix it

with your scrambled eggs. If you have any

left over, sprinkle it in your bath water.

Dissolves gritty grimy greasy rings. Mothers

love it!

(A Mother's voice:) "Sweetie, take your Triss

Germ, darling. It's going to make you grow up

to be strong and healthy like Mommy, poopsie.

Open your mouth, Precious. Come on, Lover, take

your nice Triss Germ. Honey, you're making

Mommy just a teeny weeny bit mad, Sweetums.

9

Precious Lover, you're going to make me scream.

Darling....OPEN UP, YOU ROTTEN LITTLE BEAST!"

I TRISSY

I TRISSY

I TRISSY

I TRISSY

I TRISSY

I TRISSY

We were at the table. Mother, Robert,
Mitch, and me. Mitch sat down at Daddy's place.
So I said, "Mitch, that's Daddy's place."

"Not any more," he said with a big Mouth
Watering Grin.

"Move," I said.

Just gave me another MWG.

"MOVE!"

"Stop that, Trissy," Mother said. "Mitch
can sit anywhere he wants."

"But he doesn't belong in that place." I
was so mad I was practically jumping up and
down.

"Don't raise your voice at me," Mother said.
"You respect me. I'm your mother!"

"I'm your daughter! Why don't you respect
me? Why don't you tell Mitch to get out of Daddy's
seat? Why do you always get mad at me? Why is

MITCH always right? Why am I always wrong?
What's the answer?"

"You're rude, young lady! You leave the
table and don't you come back till you are
prepared to talk and act like a civilized person."

So I left. I pounded as I went up the stairs.
I slammed the bathroom door as I passed. I
slammed the door to my room so hard the mirror
shook. Too bad it didn't fall and break into
a thousand pieces.

Now my stomach is growling. SHE wouldn't
let me eat supper. SHE wouldn't care if I died
of starvation. Probably, if SHE saw me crawling
on the desert with my bones sticking out of my
backside and my tongue hanging down to my toes,
SHE would only laugh.

Damn that Mitch.

Double damn him to hell and back. Double
damn them all, Mitch, Robert, and HER. Double

and triple and quadriple DAMN them all. To Hell

Hell Helly Hilly Hollow Hellish Hell with them

all!!

The I'll-be-glad-when-you're-dead,-Mitch-Beers

Smile:

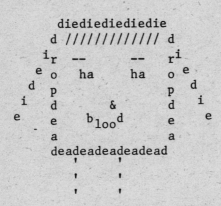

```
            diediediediedie
          d ///////////// d
        i                 i
         r  --       --   r
        e   o  ha   ha  o  e
       d    p          p    d
      i     d     &    d     i
     e      e  b   d   e      e
             loo
            a          a
            deadeadeadeadead
              '    '
              '    '
              '    '
```

```
                        ha ha
                          ha ha
                            ha
                            ha
                           hahahahahahaha
```

I, Evil to the Heart, Trissy!!!!

TO WHOM IT MAY CONCERN

I, THE UNDERSIGNED, HENCEFORTH, WILL SIT

AT THE DINNER TABLE IN MY DESIGNATED PLACE AND

EAT MY DESIGNATED FOOD WITH DESIGNATED SILVERWARE,

AND OTHERWISE CONDUCT MYSELF IN A POLITE, PERFECT,
    IR
AND XXREPROACHABLE MANNER.

EXCEPT THAT, I, THE UNDERSIGNED, REFUSE NOW

AND FOREVER, TO LOOK AT, TALK TO, OR IN ANY WAY

ACKNOWLEDGE THE PRESENCE OR EXISTENCE OF ONE

MITCH BEERS, SO LONG AS HE, MITCH BEERS, CONTINUES

TO SIT IN THE PLACE OF MY FATHER, MITCHELL POWELL

BEERS.

I DO SO SOLEMNLY SWEAR.

I, TRISSY

Mrs. Gilfer: Trissy, why do you sign all your papers 'I, Trissy'?

Trissy: I like to.

Mrs. Gilfer: But why, Trissy? You should sign your name 'Trissy Beers.'

Trissy: I like 'I Trissy' better. Is it against the law or something?

Mrs. Gilfer: Well, no, dear, and I do like to allow for your creative imagination to take its own course, but it is unusual. And then is it grammatical? Well, I believe it is, but it's a redundancy, you know?

Trissy: I don't know what that is.

Mrs. Gilfer: It says the same thing twice, Trissy. Ha ha, like 'Me, Jane.' That's a redundancy, see?

Trissy: Oh! That's why you crossed out 'huge,

enormous monster' on my tall tales
composition. But, anyway, can I
still sign my papers the way I want
to?

Mrs. Gilfer: Oh, dear. (She reached inside her
dress and straightened her straps.
Or was it her false bosoms? Everyone
says she has them.) Yes, Trissy.
You can still sign papers in my
class 'I, Trissy,' but I don't
know how your other teachers will
take it. You see what I mean?

Trissy: Thank you, Mrs. Gilfer, I will meet
that situation when it arises.
(Which is what I heard Uncle Arthur
say when he was visiting my mother.)

Mrs. Gilfer: My dear, that's very mature.

Question: Your name?

Answer: I, Trissy

18

*S*T*E*F*F*I* *J*O*N*E*S*

HAS L$_O$
       $_O$
        $_O$
         $_O$
          $_O$
           $_O$
            $_O$
             $_O$
              $_O$
               $_O$
                $_O$
                 N
                  G
                   H
                    A
                     I
                      R
AND A teentiny NOSE

                    AND A **************
                          *   *
                          * P*R*E*T*T*Y *   MOUTH
                          ****

STEFFI JONES THE TRULY BEAUTIFUL, AND TRISSY BEERS

THE TRULY BRILLIANT ARE THE GREATEST FRIENDS IN THE

WO WO WO WORLD... IN THE SO SO SO SOLAR SYSTEM....

IN THE UNI UNI UNI UNIVERSE!!!!!!

19

he he he he he he hehehehehehehehehehehehehehe

LAURA STEGMEYER IS JEALOUS

ha ha ha ha ha ha hahahahahahahahahahahahahaha

LAURA STEGMEYER KICKED TRISSY BEERS IN THE LEG

(didn't even hurt he he) BECAUSE SHE IS SO GREEN

EYED MONSTER JEALOUS OF THE GREAT WONDERFUL

TERRIFIC FANTASTIC STAR SPANGLED

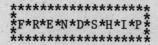

```
*******************
*                 *
*F*R*E*N*D*S*H*I*P*
*                 *
*******************
```

OF STEFFI JONES AND TRISSY BEERS.

he ha he ha he ha hehahehahehahehaheha ha ha TOO

BAD FOR YOU, LAURA STEGMEYER.

THE ITMQ TEST

The ITMQ Test (The I, Trissy Mother's
Quotient Test, devised, designed, and administered
by TJB) may be filled out by any certified child.
Use a soft pencil. Do not look at anyone else's
answers. Take 10 minutes. If you do not understan
a question, pass on to the next one, and only
return to the blanks when you have completed all
other questions.

Answer yes or no to each of the following questions
as it applies to your mother. Does she:

XXXXXXXXXXX   TRISSY   STEFFI

 1- smoke?   yes   no

 2- yell?   yes   no

 3- wear hair spray?   yes   no

 4- wear heavy makeup?   yes   no

 5- make packaged cakes?   yes   no

 6- make unpleasant remarks to   yes   no
    your father?

7- favor one or more children

above you?   yes   yes

8- fail to understand you?   yes   yes

9- get mad at you regularly?   yes   no

10- forget to rinse her mouth after

she eats garlic pickles?   yes   no

11- wear her skirts too short?   no   no

12- always flip off the tv in the

middle of your favorite show,

saying it is bedtime?   yes   no

13- act helpless when something

goes wrong with the car?   yes   yes

14- forget to come up lots of

nights to tell you goodnight?   yes   no

15- tell you you're old enough

to know better when you do

something wrong, but that

you are too young when you

22

        want to do something

        she doesn't want you to

        do and doesn't want to

        give the reason for?   yes   yes

....

Score 6 points for each NO answer. A PERFECT

ITMQ score is 90. This means you are superior

in your choise of mothers.

From 80-90: You are gifted in choice of mother.

From 70-80: You are above average in choice.

From 60-70: You fall in the average range of

            mother-choosers.

From 50-60: Disappointing.

From 40-50: Clearly a failure in mother choice.

From 20-40: Cause for alarm!

From 10-20: The situation is grave!

From 0 -10: You poor kid! How did you do it?

MEMO TO MY MOTHER

(who recently got a score of 6 in the ITMQ)

Below are a list of nine practical suggestions to improve your ITMQ test score and increase your chances of persuading my father to come live with us again. Please study each suggestion carefully and ACT on it.

1 - Stop smoking like a chimney. Your fingers and teeth are yellow, and that's ugly. You are polluting your lungs, and your children's air space, and that's bad.

2 - Look interested when my father tells stories. Don't get busy dusting or yelling at us kids. You should have done that before. And don't walk out on him in the middle of a story. Practice in front of the mirror till you know how to look interested.

3 - Get sweeter. Practice by saying nice things to your daughter, such as: What a pretty

smile!....Every day you grow more helpful!....
I'm such a lucky mother to have a daughter like
you!....

Instead of saying things like, I'm going to
scream! Your hair looks like a rat's nest!....
You could grow potatoes in those ears!....Your
room isn't fit for a pig!

4 - Stop playing favorites with your children.
Robert is NOT a baby anymore, he's going to be
seven, so stop calling him "the baby."

5 - Call up my father and tell him you're
sorry. I don't know what for. Just tell him
you're sorry for whatever it is you're sorry
for. You must be sorry for something, otherwise
he wouldn't have left us.

6 - Stop calling Mitch, "My big man." That's
disgusting, since he's only 15 years old, and
once I heard my father say you're going to get
that boy all screwed up if you don't let him off

your apron strings.

7 - Invite your husband to supper and make him a _sensational_ meal. Not hamburgers slapped on the pan when he walks in and frozen french fries in the oven, and you jumping around nervously saying, "Oh, I was so busy today, I didn't have time for anything."

8 - Bake a real cake. Not frozen strawberries glopped over store bought angel food cake that tastes like cotton. Make a real cake buried under tons of real whipped cream. Invite my father over to have coffee and cake. DON'T give Robert and Mitch bigger pieces than you give me.

9 - Last, but NOT least. Visit Steffi Jones' mother. Her mother is a real MOTHER. She is pretty, sweet, and loving. She bakes homemade cakes, smells good, and knows how to make EVERYBODY feel good. When you visit Mrs. Jones, watch EVERYTHING she does. Practice acting like

Mrs. Jones. Remember, MR. Jones is living home

with Mrs. Jones and Steffi and her little sister

Bea.

I, Trissy

AM I CREATIVE, OR FRIENDLY?

Mrs. Gilfer says, "Remember, ka-lass, kree-a-tive ex-presh-un in your compositions counts the most." She says the most kree-a-tive person in the ka-lass gets to be editor of our sixth grade yearbook.

That's sure to be Great Old Me, Beautiful Old Steffi, or (ugh) Laura Stegmeyer of the frizzy red hair.

On the playground, Ugh Stegmeyer told me I should let Beautiful Old Steffi win the contest Mrs. Gilfer opened today.

"You know how to use flashy words and will do something to draw attention to yourself," Ugh Stegmeyer said. "You say you're Steffi's best friend. Ha! You don't want her to be editor."

"It's up to Mrs. Gilfer, and depends on who's the most--"

"If I was Steffi's best friend, I would GLADLY let her win. In fact, I'm not going to hand in my very best creative effort, so Steffi can have an extra good chance." She gave me her very best creative smile and walked away.

ugh ugh ugh ugh ugh ugh ugh ugh ugh !!!!!!!!

NOTICE TO LAURA STEGMEYER

If you think you are going to get between

me and Steffi Jones by your sneaky,

insidious insinuations, you are WRONG.

If you think I am not going to do my

best CREATIVE effort in the contest,

you are WRONG AGAIN!!!!!!!!!!!!!!!!!!!!!!!!

I! Trissy!!!!!!!!

A ONCE UPON A TIME STORY

Once upon a time there lived a king and queen to whom a child was born. They named her Tolda. The king couldn't have been happier. The queen, however, couldn't be bothered, and gave the tiny princess entirely to the care of servants.

The queen was extremely high strung and screamed day and night at the king, her chief complaint being that he presented a shockingly poor image of a king. She criticized him for spending too little time sitting on the royal throne settling disputes and ordering people around. Furthermore, she accused him of being a cheapskate about keeping the royal wardrobe up to date. A real king, she scolded, didn't go around looking like a shabby last year's model.

The king, however, thought that the way he dressed was irrelevant as long as he was comfortable. And as far as the people were concerned, they didn't need to come running to him with every little problem. The king mimicked one of the supplicants.

"Oh, Dear King, Sir Lordship, Your Worship, Sir Kindness, Royal to the Highest, my father gave my brother two pairs of boots, and my brother won't share with me."

The king made a disgusted face. "Who wants to listen to a lot of boring boot licking speeches?" Besides, he said, his behind became quite numb sitting in one place for hours on <u>end</u>. "Get it!" the king chortled. "Hours on <u>end</u>!"

The queen sniffed. "You and your puns! You're a pitiful, pathetic example for the poor ignorant populace to look up to. Because of you they laugh at me!" By this time the queen had worked herself up into a fine frenzy. "Nobody respects me," she screamed. "I don't have enough money or jewels. My kingdom is filled with lazy slobs who throw stones at me when I go driving in the royal carriage."

"Now, my dear--"

"Don't you now-my-dear me, king! It's all your fault! You're not a proper king!"

"Now, Queen, don't get yourself all upset."

"'Now, Queen! Now, Queen!' Ooooh, you miserable king, you make me so angry!"

Bang! Slam! Smash! The queen didn't care who heard her kicking the royal footstools, slamming doors, and stamping her royal feet in a rage.

Nothing satisfied her. She sat on her royal throne and tapped her foot irritably. She sent the servants scurrying from one end of the palace to the other on silly errands. She was displeased

35

with everything and everyone. When her daughter
Tolda appeared, running to kiss her mother, the
queen gnashed her teeth and said, "You're too
old for that sentimental kissing stuff!" The
only person who pleased her was Sir Arthur
Suckapipe, the queen's minister, who stood behind
her throne, whispering in her ear.

It was Sir Arthur Suckapipe who gave the
queen the idea that nothing ought to satisfy her
till the king won back from the people the
respect, admiration, and fear the throne deserved.

A war, said the queen, (with Sir Arthur
Suckapipe nodding behind her) was the thing to
unite the kingdom and restore respect for the
king and queen. There was nothing like killing
the enemy to make the throne popular and the
people happy.

The king was thoroughly disgusted with this
idea. He didn't want his name connected with

killing and bloodshed. There had been too much
of that gory stuff, he said, committed in the
name of kings, kingdoms, and royal causes.

"In that case," the queen said, "you have
to set out on a long treacherous mission to find
something."

"Find what, my dear?"

"How should I know?" she screamed. "That's
your business. Surely there must be <u>something</u>
you can go out and seek!"

The king poo-pooed the idea that there was
anything beyond the kingdom that he or any of
his people needed or wanted. "We have everything
close at hand to be happy," he said.

The queen stamped her foot. "You silly
man!"

Day after day she nagged him mercilessly.
"You lazy, stay-at-home, ambitionless, big
bottomed, spineless king without a backbone!

You don't deserve the name of king!"

Finally the king became so disgusted he packed up and left. When people asked where he had gone, the queen put on her most mouth watering grin and said he had set out on a holy journey to unknown lands to win new riches and glory for their kingdoms. "Oh! Ah! How wonderful!" everyone said.

Poor Tolda. Now that her father was gone, her life became poor indeed. The queen now forced her to do palacework, spending long hours on her hands and knees mopping the mile long white marble corridors. Meanwhile the queen and Sir Arthur smiled and whispered together.

So it went for many months. Tolda grew thin and weak, her knees were red and knobby, but still she slaved. Every night she prayed for her father's safe return. Often she cried herself to sleep.

Then a strange sickness swept over the kingdom. Many people died. People whispered it was a punishment because the king was gone. They stood outside the palace, calling for the return of the king. The queen appeared in the royal robes, her crown tipsy because she had put it on in such a hurry. But the people were angry. They threw mud, stones, and slop at her. They wanted the king.

The queen was afraid. The sickness had swept to the gates of the royal household. She locked the palace doors, dismissed the gatekeeper and most of the servants. Tolda was ill and so was Sir Arthur Suckapipe. Alone and afraid, the queen shivered.

First Sir Arthur Suckapipe died. Then Tolda was taken. The queen was beside herself with remorse and grief. Now that it was too late, the queen tore her hair because she had

been so wickedly unkind to her own dearest
daughter.

But Tolda wasn't dead. Weak, her breath
almost gone, she had been carried away by the
faithful gatekeeper to a hut at the edge of a
meadow where his old mother treated her with
herbs and brought her back to life.

The queen, meanwhile, grew more and more
fearful and suspicious. The people were
whispering about her. There were rumors of a
plot afoot to oust her from the throne and
lock her in the Purple Tower. She was sorry
now she'd driven the king away. She had new
locks put on every royal door, and she allowed
no one but herself to hold the keys. She
rarely went out, but crept about the palace
muttering to herself and peering through the
cracked windows at the people outside.

One day a ragged, bearded beggar appeared

at the palace gates. The doors were locked and padlocked. There was no gatekeeper to let him in. And when he turned to the people and said he was their king, they laughed. Everyone knew the king was dead, and only a mad queen dwelt within the palace.

The queen, hearing the beggar hammering on the knax royal gates, dragged heavy wooden tables and chairs to pile against the doors, sure the revolt had begun. Thinking of her own precious head chopped off, she shivered in fear.

The king circled the palace walls. There was no response from the palace. In despair, he turned away. It was then the faithful gatekeeper found him and brought him to Tolda. There was a tearful reunion. The king showed Tolda the treasures he'd brought back, sewn in the lining of his coat. He showered diamonds, gold bracelets and silver necklaces on her.

41

Together, wearing their new treasure, they returned to the palace, raised up on the shoulders of the happy people. The queen heard the turmoil at the gates, and peering through the crack in the great door all she saw was a huge mass of shrieking, clamorous people. With a last scream, she dropped dead.

After that, the king ruled his kingdom wisely and well with Tolda at his side.

The end

I, Trissy

She met me at the door when I got home.
"I found this paper on your desk."

"What paper? Oh. That paper."

She said, "Nine practical suggestions to
improve yourself!" She was furious. She shook
the paper at me. "'Your fingers are yellow.'
Thanks, so much, my darling daughter! 'Get
sweeter.' How good of you to give me suggestions
for self improvement. I'll be ever lastingly
GRATEFUL! Now what do you have to SAY for
yourself?"

"You weren't supposed to read it."

"Oh, no! I thought it was written for my
benefit. And you thoughtfully left it right
smack on your desk so I could find it EASILY!"

"My desk is private. You had no business
snooping--"

43

WHAM! She caught me across the face. "Don't you call me a snoop besides everything else, Trissy Beers." Her voice was high and shaking. My cheek stung, and I wanted to cry, but I hated her so much I grinned instead. I grinned so hard my jaw ached. She had no right snooping. It was just something to write on my typewriter. It was my personal business.

From now on I NEVER leave anything on my desk, EVER AGAIN.

I, TRISSY

I wore my red cape to school today.

Mr. Montgomery asked me if I was practicing
to be Superwoman. "No. Superman," I said.

Everybody laughed. Mr. Montgomery didn't
like that. He likes to make the jokes. He will
get back at me for having made everybody laugh,
I know that. He's got mean eyes, but I like
his class anyway. He's always telling us bloody
stories about history. He says all of history is
written in a river of blood.

"Picture the crucified men lining the road
to Rome," he says, walking up and down in front
of the class. "Do you think Jesus was the first
or only man crucified? Fat chance. In those
days they really knew how to punish. They'd
been practicing for thousands of years, beating,
maiming, enslaving other people."

He says people used to have their hands chopped off for stealing, their ears slashed away, their noses clipped, and their eyes gouged out. He points his finger. His mean little eyes sparkle. He wakes everybody up. Nobody sleeps in Mr. Montgomery's class.

My favorite story is the one he told about Rasputin, the mad monk of Imperial Russia. His enemies wanted to kill him. They got together and poisoned his food. They were there as he ate the poisoned food. They must have been rubbing their hands together. But old Rasputin went on eating and talking. They got so mad they shot him, but he still went on living, staggering around and frightening them. Then they strangled him. He was covered with blood and gore, but still alive, gasping for breath, his huge hypnotic eyes fixed accusingly on his assassins. They were terrified. He was supposed to have

46

supernatural powers. They began to think he
would never die. Finally they threw him into
the river with weights tied to his body, and
even then he sank so slowly they thought any
moment he would come bobbing to the surface to
accuse them.

Wow.

I will now type all the words I can type using just my left hand...on my mark...get set...go!

eat ate cat rat sat sex car care west waste wad wax ax fact ass fate feet fat fast reed deed seed fart

Okay, right hand--go!

up pop pip pom pony poppy poop loop lip jim mop mom join john mill milk

Robert is pounding on the wall. That means my typewriter is bothering him. Well, too bad for little BBB Robert, my typewriter is mine own and it was given me by mine own Dad, and I can type on it all night if I wish, and you, old Robert boy, can just take your little bawling blabby baby self and bawl and blab to Mom and see where that will get you.

Here she comes now.

49

Well, I will just pretend I don't hear or notice anything, and just go on typing my fastest, with my best, most concentrated, serious working expression, and let her stand in the doorway and be mad. Sputter ~~Xuppkex~~ sputter. What does it matter to me? Ha ha the Mad Typist of Free America can not be stopped. I can type all day and type all night. I can type till my fingers fall off, and then for spite I'll still type on with my bloody stumps. Ha ha the Mad Typist strikes again. drip

dr$_i$$_p$

dr$_i$$_p$ (blood)

John Rickover came up to me on the playground today and said, "Is your name Beers?" He was finishing an ice cream pop.

"Yes, it is. Is your name Rickover?"

"You mean like Budweiser Beer?"

"No. Beers. B-e-e-r-s."

"Oh, bears," he said, making paws and growling at me.

"No, BEERS."

"You mean bare. BARE," he shouted. "B-A-R-E." He began dancing around me like an idiot, shouting, "Trissy Bare. Bare Trissy, Trissybare Trissybare. B! A! R! E! Bare BARE! BARE! BARE NAKED!"

I snatched the ice cream pop from his hand and jammed it into his mouth so hard I thought his eyes would pop out of his head. He spit it out and socked me in the shoulder. I charged him and butted him in the belly. The

51

next minute, Mr. Patterson, the playground
director, came flying over, his long legs
churning and pulled the two of us apart. Then
he gave ME a lecture. "You're a girl. Girls
aren't supposed to fight with boys--"

"Tell HIM that!" I felt like kicking
Mr. Patterson in the leg. Maybe he read my
mind. The next thing I knew I was in the
principal's office, and the secretary was
sighing, "What is it this time, Miss Trissy
Trouble?"

DEAR BLABBY,

I am always getting into trouble and lately it's worse than ever. Can you help me improve myself? My mother says I absolutely must learn to control my worst impulses. My father says I need to think twice before I speak once. And my brother Mitch says I ought to nail my feet to the floor and my mouth shut.

Right now it is Saturday. It's the day I'm supposed to spend with my father, but I am a prisoner in my room while my goody goody brothers are out with Daddy. This is my punishment for what I did yesterday on my brother Robert's birthday.

It started out to be a good day. After school Mom baked a cake for Robert instead of buying it at the Buttercup Bakery like she usually does. It was a chocolate cake (my favorite) and it looked great in the oven.

After she took it out, though, the center caved
in. My brother Mitch said that crater or not,
it was still better than any cake she could
have bought.

"Do you really mean that, Mitch?" my
mother said. "Just say the word--I'm ready
to throw it away. I honestly am."

"Oh, no, it's great. It tastes great.
Go ahead and frost it," Mitch said.

You notice she didn't ask my opinion,
which I would have been happy to give. But
for once Mitch was right and not just apple
polishing like crazy. And anyway, she let me
make the frosting and even when it came out
kind of thin and sticky, she said it was
great. I mean, it was really getting to be
a good day, even if Robert did keep pestering
everybody, "What'd you get me? Something that
cost a lot of money, I hope?"

Mom stuck seven candles in the cake, took
a roast beef out of the oven, and we all sat
down to eat. By all, I mean my mother, my
brothers, me, and Uncle Arthur. He's not our
real uncle, but Mom says calling him just
plain Arthur is disrespectful, and Mr. Jobaggy
is too formal. It's a good thing we don't
have to call him Mr. JOBAGGY, because everytime
I say Mr. JOBAGGY, I want to laugh.

Mr. JOBAGGY used to visit us sometimes
before my father left. Once I heard Daddy
call him every woman's handy neighborhood
bachelor. My father thought that was very
funny, but my mother said it was in poor taste.
Anyway, now he's at our house almost every
week, and we're supposed to be very polite
to him at all times.

I don't mind being polite (when I can
remember) but when Mom put Uncle Arthur in

55

my father's place at the table, it got me even
madder than when my brother Mitch sat there.
She didn't have to be that polite and friendly.

My mother has been pretty mad at me for
quite a long time, and I didn't want to make
her mad again, so I kept my lips sealed. I
thought of all the tortures in the world that
would happen to me if I said anything about MR.
JOBAGGY sitting in my father's place. I thought
of Chinese water torture, hanging by my thumbs,
being pulled apart limb from limb on a medieval
rack, and being pierced by steel spikes inside
the iron lady.

"What's wrong with you, Trissy?" my mother
said. "You're just picking at the food. Don't
you like the meat? I thought rare red roast
beef was your favorite."

"It's delicious," Uncle Arthur said. "I'll
take another thick, bloody piece, Edith."

"Pass Uncle Arthur the meat, Mitch," Mom
said. Mitch sneered as he passed the meat.
About the only thing Mitch and I agree on is
Uncle Arthur. We don't like him. He drawls
out his words, and takes forever to say anything.
"That's an in-ter-est-ing prob-lem," he says.
And he acts so wise and judicious. "Let's
look at the other side of the question," he
says. Which is supposed to be some kind of
wonderful, fantastic FAIR attitude to have.
Personally, I like people to have opinions.

And my opinion was that it was WRONG
for Uncle Arthur to be sitting in my father's
place, and WRONG for my father to be absent
on Robert's birthday. I was getting madder
and madder at everyone, even Robert for being
so greedy and dumb that he didn't even know
it was wrong to have his birthday without our
father.

"You're still not eating, Trissy," Mom said. She got her suspicious look, which is a sort of pinching around her nose. "Did you eat a lot of sweets and junk at school today?"

All of a sudden I made up my mind to call my father. I pushed away my plate and got a sick look on my face. That wasn't too hard. I just stared at that oozing roast beef and thought about having my eyes pulled dripping and bloody from their sockets.

"I have to go to the bathroom," I said. I was gagging. "In a rush!"

I went into the bathroom, spit into the sink, and then sort of quietly went into my mother's room. I sat on the edge of her bed, put the phone on my lap, and dialed my father's new number. A girl answered.

"Who are you?" I said.

58

"Excuse me?"

"Is this Professor Beers' residence?"

"Yes, it is," she said.

"I want to talk to him, please." I decided she was probably one of my father's students. My father is a physicist at the University, and besides teaching, he does research, and when he was living home his students used to visit him a lot.

"Hello, Tris!" he said. Just hearing his voice gave me happy shivers.

"Hello, Daddy. Can you come over to the house now? Please. Mother wants you to." I had all my fingers and both legs crossed.

"What for, Tris? I'm sort of busy. I have company--"

"Well, there's something going on, and she wants you here, because it's this family thing--"

"You mean Robert's birthday?"

"Yes, that's right. Robert's birthday.
Mom baked a cake and we're all eating now.
You've got time to get here before Robert
cuts the cake and opens his presents--"

"Well, Tris, the thing is--why? We're
going to celebrate Robert's birthday again,
when I see you kids tomorrow. I have a
pretty nice special treat planned for you and
your brothers. Your mother and I agreed--"

"Robert wants you," I said. "He wants
you so bad, he's crying. He's really crying
hard."

"You mean Robert is crying?" Dad said.

"Yes. He's crying BUCKETS! I feel so
sorry for him." I got tears in my eyes. I
get that way when I tell a story. It seems
so real to me, I forget I'm making it all up.

"The worst thing is, Mom is getting mad at him for ruining his birthday celebration. She spent a lot of time baking a real cake, and now he's acting so sad and babyish because you're not here."

Dad must have put his hand over the phone because I didn't hear him breathing or anything for a minute. Then he came back again and said, "Okay, I'll be right over, Tris. You tell Robert I'll be right over and to stop crying. In about ten, fifteen minutes, okay?"

I went back to the table. I felt sort of tense at what I'd done. Mom frowned. "Where were you so long, Trissy?" Because of Uncle Arthur, she kept her voice sweet. "Were you in the bathroom all this time?"

"I thought you fell in," Mitch said.

"And got flushed away," Robert yelled.

"Oh, boy, funn-y," I said.

I was getting to feel more and more peculiar thinking about what I'd done, about Dad's coming over, and how surprised everyone was going to be, especially Mom. She kept giving me these penetrating looks, which meant she was wondering if my stomach was still upset. Usually when I stay in the bathroom too long, she wants to know if I am all right, or if I have cramps, and did I have a normal movement.

And if I didn't, then out comes the stuff which gets you tightened right up. I hate it. It tastes like chalk, but Mom always makes me take four huge tablespoonsful which make me feel sicker than any cramps. Anyway, I think it is disgusting that a person my age still has to answer humiliating personal questions.

My stomach had been growling and working ever since I made the phone call. Suddenly I burped. It was very loud, like this UUURRRP

and came so fast I didn't have time to cover my
mouth.

Mom gave me a freezing what-horrible-manners
look. Mitch snickered in a superior way even
though he burps all the time himself, and MUCH
louder and more vulgar than I could ever hope
to be. (He wins every burping contest hands
down.)

About then, Dad walked in. "Why, Mitchell,"
my mother said. "What are you doing here? I
thought we agreed you'd call before you came
over--"

When my father and Uncle Arthur saw each
other, both their faces got red and stiff. "What
do you mean?" my father said. "Trissy called
me and said you wanted--" He looked at Robert.
"She said the boy was crying for me."

Everyone looked at me.

"I think I'll go to the bathroom," I said.

"Sit down!" my mother ordered.

"I wasn't crying," Robert said. "Why would I cry? It's my birthday, and I'm happy because I'm getting a big bunch of presents that cost a lot of money."

"Just exactly what did you have in mind, Trissy?" my mother said.

"You lied to me," Daddy said. "Robert wasn't crying."

"Me cry? I never cry," Robert said cheerfully.

"Don't you think 'lie' is a little strong, Mitchell?" Uncle Arthur said. "She's only a child. Her motives, I'm sure, were well intended--"

"Keep out of this," my father said. "What are you doing here anyway?" Uncle Arthur stood up. Then my father said, "Oh, forget it, will you, Art?"

"Honestly!" my mother said. "Honestly!"
I couldn't tell if she was madder at me or at
my father.

"Well, Dad," Mitch said, "why don't you
sit down, now that you're here, and have cake
with us, anyway?" I almost fell off my chair.
For once in my life I could have kissed old
Mitch, even if he is 15, and you know that is
a smelly age for boys. I mean, their underarm
perspiration odor is enough to knock you dead
at 20 paces.

Dad sat down. Robert made his greedy,
dollar sign face and asked if Dad had brought
his birthday present. Mom ordered me to clear
the plates and wipe the table. She brought in
the cake. Uncle Arthur clapped. No one else
did.

Robert couldn't blow out the candles alone,
and Mitch and Dad and Uncle Arthur all had to

help him. "All together now," Uncle Arthur

said. "One big blow!" Out went the candles

and everyone started talking, while Robert

ripped open his presents.

"Happy Birthday, Robert," I x yelled,

thinking that people weren't xxx mad at me

anymore.

But parents never forget. My punishment

for lying to Dad, deceiving Mom, and generally

being disruptive is not being allowed to go out

with my father today and being confined to my

room all day. My parents agreed on this punishment.

I think it's fantastically dumb that the ONLY thing

they have actually agreed on in months is how

terrible I am, and what my punishments should be.

But when I tried to say so, Mom told me I'd said

enough and more than enough.

I have tired out my fingers, but made two

hours pass writing all this to you, Dear Gabby,

and now my fingers are just going by themselves,
and they are almos nummmm now and i am tootired
to use capitolletters anymore and i gess i
will strt shrt handng all mi splng becuz it
is 2 much trbl 2 kp rting evree thng out

i evn hav 2 lok back 2 rembr wat my kweshtun
wuz. sumthng abot beng a betr persn. do u
thnk u can anser that nd also giv me sum
pontrs on kping out of trbl?

sinfly yrs

don in the moth

i trissy

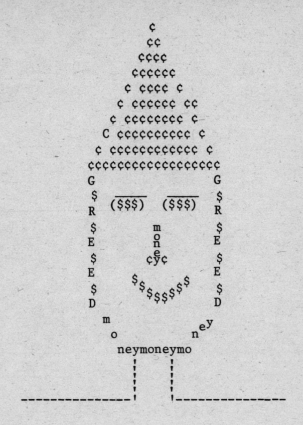

RED, WHITE, & BLUE

A play in three acts

by

T. J. Beers

ACT I

Setting: The Jefferson Elementary School

Scene: Classroom, Monday morning.

The teacher, MR. MONTGORY, sits on the edge of

his desk, flipping a piece of chalk from one hand

to the other. In front of him sit his students.

That is, some of them are sitting, some are

talking, some are reading funny books. The

bell rings. Everyone jerks to attention. In

the front row sits MELISSA SNEERS. Next to

her, her best friend, STEFFI PRETTY. Directly

behind Steffi Pretty sits Melissa Sneers worst,

most hated enemy, LIAR STEWMIAR.

Melissa Sneers is wearing a navy blue skirt,

71

white blouse, red cape, and one red sock, one
white sock. Melissa Sneers has a reason for
dressing this way. Over the weekend, Melissa
was severely and unjustly punished by her cruel
guardians. Now she is protesting. Red stands
for anger. White for innocence, and blue for
unjust punishment.

Melissa sits with the cape wrapped around herself.
She is behaving perfectly, bothering no one with
her silent red, white, and blue protest.

MR. MONTGORY: Melissa Sneers, remove your cape.

MELISSA: (standing) I don't wish to remove
                my cape, Mr. Montgory.

(Melissa is utterly polite. Everyone in the class
sits up and watches. They now expect some fun
from Mr. Montgory, who is renowned for his
sarcastic manner.)

MR. MONTGORY: Miss Sneers, if it is not too much
                trouble, I expect you to comply with

my orders in this classroom. Now,

if Miss Sneers does not mind walking

back to the cloak room, I and all

the others in this class would be

most appreciative if Miss Sneers

removed her cape and hung it with

other garments designed for wear

OUTSIDE the classroom.

(Appreciative snickers from the students. Melissa
bravely holds her ground and her cape.)

MR. MONTGORY: Melissa Sneers, you are being

DISRUPTIVE!

MELISSA: (aghast at such unfairness) Mr.

Montgory, would you say I was being

disruptive if I had a flag?

MR. MONTGORY: I don't see what that has got to

do with anything, Miss Sneers!

MELISSA: If I had a flag, it would be the

same colors as the colors I am

wearing, and everybody would stand

and salute.

(At this, John Lickover stands and salutes Melissa

Sneers. All students scream with laughter,

except Steffi Pretty, who looks very pale, ladylike,

and angry with her best friend, Melissa Sneers,

for causing such a commotion.)

MR. MONTGORY: Melissa Sneers, do you refuse to

take off your cape?

MELISSA: (bravely) Yes, Mr. Montgory, I

refuse.

MR. MONTGORY: Miss Sneers, I will give you one

more chance! Take off your cape!

MELISSA: Mr. Montgory, if I take off my cape,

I will take off my skirt and blouse

also, because they are an outfit and

all three go together.

(At this, boys stamp their feet and laugh, girls

giggle, and Steffi Pretty looks even paler and

angrier.)

MR. MONTGORY: Melissa Sneers, go to the office

                    IMMEDIATELY!

(Melissa Sneers exits, proudly holding the red

cape around herself. Students look after her,

buzzing. Mr. Montgory raps on desk for order.)

                    Curtain falls.

                        ACT II

Setting: Office of the Principal of Jefferson

Elementary school. There is a barred window

over the reception desk. Several student prisoners

sit on a bench waiting for their cases to be

called. They are a tough looking bunch. Into

their midst comes Melissa Sneers with her red

cape sailing behind her. Everyone gasps at the

bold, striking picture she makes as she sits

down. Much whispering behind hands. They are

pointing her out as the girl who defied Mr.

Montgory and threatened to take off her blouse

                        75

and skirt in his class.

SECRETARY: (looking disapprovingly through

                      the barred window) You may go

                      in now, Melissa Sneers.

(Melissa rises and sweeps her cape about her.

The door to the Principals's Office swings

silently open. Melissa enters.)

                      Curtain falls.

                      ACT III, Scene I

Setting: (That same afternoon.) Girls Locker

Room. Melissa Sneers, Steffi Pretty, Liar

Stewmiar in blue gym suits, ready to enter gym.

LIAR STEWMIAR: Well, Melissa? What happened?

                      What did Mr. Anderwert say? What's

                      he going to do to you?

MELISSA: Do? We talked for a while. I

                      explained the situation, and he

                      agreed it's my right to dress the

                      way I want to. He gave me permission

to wear my cape in school.

(Liar and Steffi gasp.)

LIAR STEWMIAR: You must be lying!

MELISSA: (coldly) I never lie. I always

                 tell the utter truth!

STEFFI PRETTY: Well, I think you made a fool

                 of yourself in class today!

                 Come on, Liar.

(She and Liar link arms and leave for gym,

leaving Melissa behind.)

                 Curtain falls.

                 ACT III, Scene 2

Setting: The gymnasium. Parallel bars. A rope

hanging from the ceiling. It is Melissa Sneers'

turn to climb the rope. MR. MUSCLES, the gym

teacher, blows his whistle.

MR. MUSCLES: Halfway up the rope, girls!

(Steffi Pretty and Liar Stewmiar have just come

down and are standing together, rubbing their

sore hands and arms. Melissa Sneers starts up
the ropes. She gets to the halfway mark.)

MR. MUSCLES: That's just fine, Melissa. You

can come down now.

(Melissa keeps going, hand over hand, feet
clutching the rope. Up, up, and up to the very
top, where she dangles with one hand as the
entire girls' sixth grade gym class gasps in
disbelief.)

MR. MUSCLES: Terrific, Melissa! Girls, all

you girls, look at Melissa. Look

at what any of you girls could

do if you tried harder. Great,

Melissa! Okay, come on down now.

(Melissa slides down the ropes. Steffi Pretty
comes up to her as they are lining up for the
next exercises.)

STEFFI PRETTY: What's the matter with you,

Melissa Sneers?

You are getting unbelievable,

lately. You are such a showoff,

I can't stand it. Do you have to

show off for EVERY man teacher in

the WHOLE school?

LIAR STEWMIAR: (who has listened to everything)

She can't help it. She's crazy.

I mean, MAN crazy.

(Liar Stewmiar and Steffi Pretty giggle. Melissa

pretends she doesn't care. She smiles hard at

Steffi Pretty. Melissa's stomach grumbles and

growls. Suddenly a burp comes into Melissa's

throat. She tries to hold it back. She can't.

She burps loudly.)

STEFFI PRETTY: You're disgusting!

(Steffi Pretty and Liar Stewmiar put their arms

around each other. Melissa Sneers, standing

alone, looks sadly after them.)

Curtain falls.

The end.

HOW TO GET LOST, FIND A NEW FRIEND,

AND MAKE YOUR ENTIRE FAMILY FURIOUS

Saturday, when Daddy picked us up, he hugged me, so I knew he wasn't mad about Robert's birthday anymore. And he had me sit in front next to him, with Mitch and Robert in back. Robert was jumping around and talking, but Mitch was sitting in the corner, looking out the window with his chin in his hands, looking gloomy and stiff like he hated being in the car with Dad. And when Dad talked to him, Mitch kept answering everything with one word.

"Well, Mitch, how was school this week?"

"Okay."

"Okay. What do you mean by that? Did you keep up with all your classes this week?"

"Sorta."

"Well, how about math? You're taking eleventh grade math this year, right?"

"Yeah."

"Well, how's that going?"

"Okay."

"That's trig, isn't it?"

"Yeah."

"Trig's not easy."

"Yeah."

"You've got to keep up with the work, not fall behind."

"Uh-huh."

"Are you having any trouble with this, Mitch?"

"Nuh."

And so on like that, with Mitch just grunting out one word answers. Mean, just plain mean. When Daddy asked me about school, I told him everything I could think of, even about Mrs. Gilfer and her false bosoms. Dad laughed and glanced back at Mitch. Old Happy Face didn't

even crack a smile. I was really mad at him.
We only see our father once a week, so it's
just mean of Mitch to act like a grim old grouch
head.

At the museum, where Daddy took us, Mitch
didn't act any nicer. He leaned against the
wall and yawned and yawned. Robert ran up and
down the spiral ramp, and Dad and I looked at
the pictures. Almost every weekend Dad brings
us to the museum. It's getting kind of boring,
but I wouldn't hurt his feelings by saying so.
Some of the pictures are really weird. There's
one that's purple and green and goes in and
out as you watch it. It's the design that
gives you that feeling, Dad said. When you
turn away, you've got purple and green spots
in front of your eyes, and everything's going
in and out, in and out, like a swinging door.
It's one of my favorite pictures.

"I guess Mitch is bored," Dad said as we went on to another picture.

"This is _fun_," I said. Dad put his arm around my shoudler. "I _love_ the museum," I said. "Let's not miss a single Saturday!"

"Well, sure, if that's the way you feel, Tris. But right now, I think we better find something to do that Mitch likes, also."

Dad motioned to the door, and Mitch sort of slouched out after us. "What now?" he said, sounding like he was ready to pass out from boredom.

"I was thinking--maybe the boat show at the War Memorial?" Dad said.

"Yeah. Three cheers for the boat show," Robert yelled.

"I don't like boat shows," I said. Dad wasn't listening. He was watching Mitch.

"That's a pretty good idea," Mitch said,

like he was a prince, handing out a favor to a
mere subject.

"I thought you'd go for the boat show,"
Dad said with a happy look on his face. Mitch
had wanted a sailboat for years. Before he left
us, Dad said he might get our family a sailboat
this summer.

"I don't like boat shows," I said again.
But Mitch and Dad were already leading the way
to the War Memorial. Robert was running around
them, shooting his finger at the pigeons bobbing
around on the sidewalk. Robert thinks it's
funny to scare them up into the air. I told
him pigeons have feelings, too, and maybe even
have nervous breakdowns from being scared by
dumb kids who yell at them and scatter them.

"Huh, Smarty," he said, "what about cars?
They make a trillion times more noise than I
do."

I walked behind him. The sun was hot. The sidewalk was gritty and cruddy. I had this peculiar itching feeling all over. Dad and Mitch turned the corner. Robert followed them. Dad had his arm around Mitch's shoulder, and they were walking in step. I kept walking along, looking down at the sidewalk. If you look carefully, you can see lines and tracks all over. They're like secret signals. They're saying, follow me, follow me, follow meeeeeeeeeee.

I guess I just walked right by the corner where Dad had turned because I was so busy following the tracks. I crossed a street, turned a corner, and kept following. Lines opened up into more lines. I followed one path through a grassy lot and came out behind a big building. There was a wooden fence, trash cans, and a rusty mattress spring. I looked up at the wall of the building. It was

an office building with green windows all up
and down its face. I wondered if someone had
thrown the rusty mattress spring down from one
of those green windows.

It was about then I realized I had got
myself lost. I followed my grass track out to
the street again. Dad and Mitch and Robert
were nowhere around, and I was in a part of
the city I'd never been in before. Right
next to the new office building with green
windows was a huge lot with nothing on it but
a big billboard that said Urban Renewal. Some
kids were playing ball in a corner of the lot.
I found some tracks in the dirt and kept
following them. I was in the section of town
where black people live. Across the street
was a housing development, rows and rows of
three story brick houses with little squares
of green in front, and clothes lines and garbage

pails on the concrete courtyards in back.

Kids were playing everywhere. Some mothers were out in the backyards hanging clothes or talking or yelling at their little kids. Quite a few men had the hoods of their cars up and were working on them. Boys on bikes rode past me in herds.

"Out of the way, white girl!" one of them yelled, and he rode so close he snatched my beret and dropped it to the ground. Then he and all his friends he-hawed like a bunch of donkeys. Boys. I stuck out my tongue at them and plunked my beret back on my head. It's red to match my cape.

If I'd had somebody to walk with, I would have felt really happy. Around our neighborhood, there are kids fooling around, but not nearly as many as here, and you hardly ever see the grownups outside, just when they come out to start up the power mowers and do the lawns, or go shopping, or something. But where I was, there was something to look at every minute.

I stopped in a little store on the corner and bought a candy bar. Then somebody yelled my name.

"Trissy! Hey, Trissy baby!" It was Patricia Crosby, one of the bus kids in my classroom. She's a dark, tall skinny girl with glasses. "What are you doing here, baby?" she said.

"Walking around."

She put her arm through mine. "Well, I'll walk with you. Where you going?"

"No place special. Just walking and looking."

"Looking at what?" she said. She sounded mad all of a sudden.

"Everything," I said. I held out my candy

bar. "Want a bite?"

"I'm allergic to chocolate," she said. "Also strawberries. I break out in a rotten rash. I itch everywhere, even on my behind."

That made me think of a funny story about my uncle Frank--the time he was out fishing and decided to take a swim and sat down in a patch of poison ivy to pull off his pants.

So we were both laughing, and Patricia said, "Maybe we'll be friends."

"Maybe," I said. It's hard to be friends with someone who lives across the city from you.

"Want to eat lunch with me and Dolores on Monday?" Patricia asked.

I thought about Steffi. Ever since she said those things in gym class, she and Laura Stegmeyer had gone everywhere and done everything together. But maybe by Monday she would want to be friends again. What would I do then?

"I asked you something," Patricia said.
She sounded mad again.

"Yes, let's eat lunch together on Monday,"
I said, and I was sorry I had hesitated because
Patricia didn't sound as friendly again. Even
so, we had a good time, walking around, talking
about everyone and everything in school. She
told me she would like school a lot better if
there were at least a few black teachers. I
had never thought of that before, and I tried
to imagine what it would be like for me to be
in a school with all black teachers, and no
white teachers. I decided that it shouldn't
make any difference, but it probably would.

"How're you getting home?" she said at
last.

"I don't know if I ought to go home, or
go back downtown and try to find my father."
I tried to explain to Pat how I'd wandered away

91

from them, following the signs and tracks.

"You've got problems," she said, making
the crazy sign on her forehead.

Right then, I realized I really did have
problems. Daddy was probably boiling over right
that instant.

"Why don't you go downtown--, it's not that
far from here," Pat said. "Then you can find
your pop or else take a bus home. Wait till I
ask my mom if it's okay, and I'll walk you part
way." I went to her house and waited outside
while she checked with her mother. She came out,
eating an apple and carrying one for me.

She walked me all the way back to the
library, then she went home, and I went to the
War Memorial. It looked like about a million
people milling around, going in to see the
show, and another million coming out from
seeing the show. I stood on my toes and swung

92

my head back and forth, looking for Dad and Mitch and Robert, till my neck ached. It cost me a dollar to get into the show, and I didn't have that much money. I had 50 cents, though, and when I couldn't see Dad or my brothers anywhere, I went to Woolworths and bought a hot dog. I wanted ice cream, too, but I needed bus fare home.

I always like taking the bus. I sat at a window and watched everything moving by. The starts and stops, the rumbles, creaks, and groans of the bus, the skeek, skeek of the doors opening and then shutting with a hot hissss made me feel goofy and a little bit sick and sort of floaty at the same time. And these goofy crazy things all tumbled around in my mind.

At the stop near my house, the driver said, "Okay, kid, are you getting off or not?" Because I was thinking, maybe I ought to keep

riding the bus for a while more. But I got off.
I stopped at the school playground. Some little
kids were on the swings. I thought about showing
them how to stand up and pump yourself so high
your feet point straight at the sky.

A boy was trying to get a kite up into the
air. "Run, you dodo," I yelled. But he just
dumbly kept flopping the kite along the ground.

If I'd had my jump rope, I would right
then and there have jumped 200 times without
missing.

But I had to go home.

Everyone was waiting for me. And they all
stared at me when I walked in. "WHERE WERE YOU?"
my mother said.

"She had candy," Robert said. "I can see
chocolate on her face."

"We were getting ready to call the police,"
Dad said.

Only Mitch kept his mouth shut, just leaned against the wall with his arms folded, smirking his superior smirk.

I tried to explain what happened, but no matter what I said, they got mad. "You went into _that_ section," Mom said. "Don't you have ANY sense?"

"Huh?" I said.

"Edith, let's not get into your narrow minded viewpoint," Dad said.

"Then you condone what she did?"

"No, I don't condone it! I'm good and mad at this girl. It was one of her typically senseless actions. She had me pretty worried! Well, Trissy Jane, what did you expect to prove--in this thoughtless way--your independence or some other half-baked notion?"

"I told you, I just started following lines--tracks--"

"Har, har, har," Mitch said. "I told you she was cracked."

"Shut up! Make him shut up!"

"That's enough out of you, Mitch," Dad said. "You and Robert leave the room. Now, Trissy Jane. What are we going to do with you? You don't think you can get away scot free with this kind of behavior, do you?"

"Do you want to beat me?"

"Don't be stupid! Just sit there with your mouth shut for a change." After a lot more talk, he and Mom decided to suspend my allowance for a month this time, and give me more chores around the house. One of these days they're going to run out of punishments, and then what are they going to do?

DREAM NUMBER I

Last night I dreamed about Steffi's mother.
In the dream she was wearing a beautiful blue
dress and she had baked a huge orange cake for
me. The cake had four candles on it for my
birthday. Then Steffi wanted the cake, but her
mother said NO, it was mine. Her mother's hair
was long and floaty like Steffi's and she hugged
me. Then I jumped into the cake and it was
soft and squishy and everybody was laughing
and feeling good.

When I woke up I felt so happy I wanted
to visit Steffi's mother right away. But first
I had to ask my mother's permission. I have
to ask her permission for EVERYTHING from now
on, because of wandering away from Dad and my
brothers.

Uncle Arthur was over and he and Mom were
talking about taking a ride. "Trissy, why

don't you come with us?" Uncle Arthur said.
He took his pipe out of his mouth and smiled
his keen friendly smile.

"No, thank you, Uncle Arthur. I want to
visit a friend."

"My, how polite," my mother said. "What
are you up to today, Trissy?" She looked at
Uncle Arthur and laughed. He laughed his keen
friendly laugh.

"Can I go over to the Jones'?" I said.

"May I?" my mother said.

"May I go over to the Jones'?"

"Well, I guess you'll be all right for a
few hours. But no repeat performances on
yesterday!"

"Yesterday. What happened yesterday?"
Uncle Arthur said.

"Oh, Trissy went off and got herself lost
and threw us all into a panic. Typical Trissy

stuff. I tell you, I was shaking till she walked in that door." Then she put her hand on my head and sort of messed up my hair in a friendly way.

INSTRUCTIONS ON MAKING UP WITH YOUR BEST FRIEND

1. Make the first move.

This is VERY important. Swallow your pride, smile and say something friendly like, "You're wearing a neat dress, Steffi!" Even though you're in her house and she doesn't answer, keep smiling in a really friendly way.

2. Don't make dumb jokes about your friend's new friend.

There must be <u>something</u> about Laura Stegmeyer that's nice. Her frizzy orange hair? Her speckled yellow eyes? Or the way she squints in that keen, super intelligent way?

3. Let your friend be FIRST in everything.

Even when her own mother asks you to choose the first piece of candy, politely decline. "Steffi can go first." Do the same thing in school. Don't wave your hand in Mrs. Gilfer's face. Give Steffi a chance to answer FIRST.

4. Give up something you really want for friendship's sake.

Give up trying to be editor of the sixth grade yearbook. Maybe lots of people, including Steffi's own mother, have told you you would be a good editor, so what? Try not to smile like an idiot when people say those things, and instead point out that Steffi knows how to get along with people a million times better than you.

5. Use every opportunity to be friendly and helpful to your friend.

Remember, friends laugh at the things you laugh at, they like the things you like, they're happy when you're happy, and sad when you're sad. Friends are the best things a person can have. So MAKE UP with your best friend, NO MATTER WHAT!

Dialogue from Real Life

Setting: Playfound during recess.

Trissy: Hi, Steffi.

Steffi: Hi.

Trissy: Patricia and I were just going across

the street to the candy store. You

and Laura want to come?

Steffi: There isn't enough time. The bell's

going to ring in a minute. I love your

dashiki, Patricia.

Trissy: Those cookies your mother made yesterday

when I was visiting were fabulous.

Steffi: Laura and I had them for lunch today.

See, there's the bell ringing. Wait

a minute, Trissy, let Pat and Laura and

the others go ahead. I want to ask you

something.

Trissy: You DO?

Steffi: Why did you come to my house yesterday?

Trissy: To see your mother. I like your mother.

And to see you, too.

Steffi: I think you came to spy on me.

Trissy: What?

Steffi: You heard me. You came to spy, to see

if Laura was over playing with me.

Trissy: I wouldn't care if Laura played with

you every day and every night for the

rest of the year.

Steffi: Why did you follow me all over my house

and give me all those sickening smiles?

Trissy: I wouldn't care if Laura Stegmeyer moved

in with you. Laura Stegmeyer. Ha. What's

Laura Stegmeyer to me? Nothing!

Steffi: You're jealous of Laura Stegmeyer. You're

so jealous it sticks out all over your

jealous green face.

Trissy: Jealous of Laura Stegmeyer? Ha, ha, ha, ha!

Steffi: And while I'm at it, I might as well tell

you I think the way you act in school is

disGUSting. You are always showing off

and lying. Like today, telling Mrs.

Gilfer in front of the whole class you

didn't want to be class editor. You gave

her one of your sickening smiles, and I

know WHY. You were just lying, pretending

to be so modest so Mrs. Gilfer would be

impressed. I think it was a disGUSting

trick!

Trissy: It was not a trick! I meant every word,

but NOW I take it all back.

Steffi: Naturally! Because the truth is, you

want to be class editor so bad you'd get

down on your hands and knees in front of

the whole world and BEG for it.

Trissy: Ha! Ha! The way YOU hang around Mrs.

Gilfer makes me want to PUKE. All that

extra work you hand in. Your greedy

ambition to be class editor sticks out

all over your greedy green face.

Steffi: Your voice is loud and UGLY, and you're

always raising your hand and waving it

in front of everyone else. I don't care

what you say about me, I'm just telling

you all this for your own GOOD, because

we used to be best friends.

Trissy: I think you are the rottenest ASS I

ever knew.

Steffi: That's another thing. Your disGUSting

language. You're always saying disGUSting

things just so you can make the boys laugh.

And the way you dress! Different colored

socks and--

Trissy: My socks are the same color today!

Steffi: ...and that cape you are always showing

off in, and everything else. I really

can't stand you, anymore.

Trissy: I not only can't stand you, you ASS, I

hate you. Goodby.

Steffi: Goodby! And good riddance to bad rubbish.

You are POLLUTION, and please don't ever

come near me again.

Trissy: May God strike me DEAD if I ever do.

THE MAD BAD TYPIST STRIKES AGAIN

and again!!!

evil words everywhere!!!

ass ass ASS ASSASS ASSSSSSSS

fark farkfarkfarkfark FARK F-A-R-K!

falling from the clouds...chalked on the sidewalks...

oh those EVIL WORDS...he he he...painted on the

sides of buildings...squigling down dark hallways...

sneaking around corners...

making mothers SHRIEK

and nicey nicey girls FAINT

oh phooey i hate my evil self

i'm going to see my father

RIGHT NOW!

Mom's gone to the market. Robert's with her.

Mitch is supposed to be watchdogging me. bow wow.

He's downstairs with the teevee.

I'm supposed to ask him if I want to go somewhere.

Rats on that.

I think if a daughter wants to see her father,

she ought to be able to go see him without asking

permission, or calling, or doing anything so

dumb. She ought to be able to just go see

her father.

so I'm going.

Report to the President from Secret Agent ITJB

Subject:

How Secret Agent ITJB got into her

father's locked apartment.

What Secret Agent ITJB did in her father's

apartment.

Why Secret Agent ITJB went beserk before

she left.

THIS MEMO IS HIGHLY CONFIDENTIAL.

SECRET   SECRET   SECRET

SECRET   SECRET   SECRET

Secret Agent ITJB left her home at exactly 3:42

p.m. and proceeded to Oak Street, where her father

now resides. She walked 57 blocks and by the time

she rang the doorbell of Mitchell Beers in the

downstairs hall, her feet really hurt.

Oooh, did they ever. And what was worse--all

111

the way over, I was thinking Dad would give me a ride home, and then he didn't even answer the bell. I kept ringing and ringing. I didn't want to walk home 57 blocks. I rang some more. Suddenly this guy with wiry hair came charging out into the hall, yelling. "Knock it off, kid! Knock it off!"

I said I was here to see my father and he lived in this house.

He said, "Go see the super and stop ringing that stupid bell!"

So I rang the bell that said superintendent. A baldheaded man answered the door. "Yesss?" he said. He had a toothpick in the corner of his mouth.

"Excuse me," I said, "I'm Mitchell Beers' daughter and he isn't home. I want to wait for my father. Do you know who could let me into his apartment?"

112

"Yessss." He flipped the toothpick from one end of his mouth to the other.

"Well, could you tell me who that is?"

"Yessssss."

"Who is it, please?"

"Me."

"Well, would you please let me in?"

He folded his arms across his chest. "Why?"

"Why what?"

"Why should I let you in?"

I was beginning to think that everyone in this house was slightly crazy. "Because I'm Mitchell Beers' daughter and he isn't home, and I'd like to go into his apartment and wait for him!"

"How do I know you're really Beers' daughter? Maybe you're a thief."

"ME?" I nearly screeched. I was so mad I stamped my foot, even though it was a truly

juvenile thing to do. I went to the door and
yanked it open, thinking about those 57 blocks
I had to walk back home, and how the whole trip
had been a big fat ZERO.

"Hey, Beers' daughter. Come on!" He
twitched his finger at me. He jungled a bunch
of keys on a metal ring. "I'll let you in."

I followed him up the stairs, and I started
hearing this story in my head. Once upon a time,
Trissy went to see her father, and this mad killer
disguised as the janitor let her in.

By the time we got to a really dark part
of the hall, I was afraid it was going to be
goodby, Trissy.

He put his clammy hands with the filthy
long nails around her slender neck, and squeezed....

"Mr. Christopher!" A woman wearing pink
fuzzy bedroom slippers, with pink rollers in her
hair, popped out of her apartment. "Mr.

114

Christopher! Just the man I want to see!"

"Busy now," the super said.

"But, Mr. Christopher," Pink Lady pouted,
"you promised to look at my sink a whole week
ago. It leaks constantly!"

"Busy now," he said again. He turned
the corner and twitched his finger at me.

"But Mr. Christopher!"

I followed him up the next flight, thinking
that Pink Lady had saved me from being strangled
on the second floor, but who was going to save
me on the third floor?

_Ha_, _ha_, _ha_, _the_ _mad_ _killer_ _laughed_ _hollowly_.
Trissy _tried_ _to_ _scream_, _but_ _everything_ _was_ _turning_
black.

"Beers' daughter!" He was holding open a
door. "This is it."

I slid in past his outstretched arm. _Just_
when _she_ _thought_ _she_ _was_ _safe_, _he_ _lunged_ _for_ _her_

soft exposed throat. "Thanks," I sort of squeaked.

He nodded. "Tell your Daddy it was your idea to have me let you in. And, Beers' daughter, if you don't wait for him, be sure to lock when you go out." He shut the door.

I looked around. I'd been in my father's apartment only once before when he first moved in. I'd wanted to come again, but there was always some reason I couldn't. Either he was busy, or Mom said I was, or he said everything was in a mess and no place for a girl.

There were newspapers spread on the navy blue couch. First I sat down. I picked up a newspaper. Then I put it down and looked around some more. I hummed to myself. I noticed an ashtray practically choking with cigarette butts. I picked up a butt and stuck it in my mouth. Then some of the tobacco got on my tongue and tasted really bad. I spit it out and wondered when Dad would be home. Then I got the idea of cleaning up.

I jumped up and folded all the newspapers neatly together and stacked them on a corner table. I emptied three ashtrays and wiped them clean with the sleeve of my sweater. There were books everywhere, even on the floor. I gathered them up and stacked them into the bookcase near the hall door.

After that I went into the bedroom. It was as bare as the livingroom. A bed, a bureau, and two chairs. No curtains, no rugs, no pictures on the walls. Just Dad's hairbrush and some loose change on the bureau. I got a sad feeling, thinking how pretty everything is at home. I wondered if Dad missed it. I pulled up the shade and looked out the window. Down on the street, there were cars, cars, and more cars. And Dad always said he hated traffic.

I went into the bathroom. I opened the medicine cabinet and took down Dad's jar of Noxema, which he uses for shaving. I liked the smell. Since he moved out, I really miss that smell. Mitch doesn't have any beard yet, and when he does grow one, he'll probably be so contrary he wouldn't use Noxema for shaving if you offered him a million dollars.

The sink didn't look too clean, but I really hate scrubbing sinks. Mom's always trying to get me to scrub the bathroom sink, or the kitchen sink. I looked at the can of cleanser, sprinkled a little on the sink, yawned, and put the cleanser back under the sink. I ran water and swished it around. Even for my father, I didn't see what difference it made if the sink was clean or not.

Next I decided to go into the kitchen. There's always dishes, pots, and things to wash

or wipe in a kitchen. I don't like washing
dishes either, but if I did Daddy's dishes, he'd
see how useful I could be. Then he'd say, "Why,
Trissy, now I know what's been missing in my
life. YOU. Why don't you come live with me?"

I was so struck by this perfect idea that
I stopped dead in the doorway between the livingroom
and the kitchen so I could see the whole thing
happening in my mind. I could see Dad's face
and the way he'd push his hand back over his head
when he said it. "Why, Trissy! What's the matter
with me? I must have been blind all these months!
You have to come live with me. Your mother has
the two boys, so she won't be lonely. It's only
fair that I have at least one of my children!"
Then he'd whisper in my ear, "Anyway, you were
always my favorite. Of all the children, I've
missed YOU the most. Yes, the very most."

I felt so bubbly and light thinking that,

119

I decided I would wash a whole sinkful of dishes,
and then go into the bathroom and scrub the sink
and the tub, too!

Then I saw the cake.

It was set in the middle of the kitchen
table, a two layer cake with chocolate fudge
frosting running down the sides. I didn't touch
it. I bent close and sniffed. It smelled fresh.
All along, I had wondered what that good smell
in the apartment was. There was a folded note
slipped under the plate the cake was on. I
picked it up and read it.

"MITCHY,

I came down with a severe case of
domesticity this morning and decided
I should do something positive with
it. Let myself in and cleaned up the
kitchen. Still feeling positively
domestic. Hence, freshly baked,

homemade (NO mixes!) cake. Hope you

like it!!!!!!!!!

Call me tonight.

Yours, G."

I folded the note very carefully and put
it back where I found it. I didn't plan to go
out of my mind. I didn't do it on purpose.
It just happened.

I plunged both hands into the cake, all
ten fingers. The cake was still warm inside.
I squeezed and mashed it until it was all over
the table top. Then I gathered gobs of chocolate
fudge frosting in my hands. I smeared hand prints
of frosting on the kitchen walls, through the
livingroom, and out into the hall. Maybe I was
laughing when I did it. Maybe I was crying. I
thought, <u>Boy, this sure is a disgusting mess</u>,
but I couldn't stop. I even smeared fudge frosting
on the bannister going down the stairs. Then I
walked home. 57 blocks.

MEDICAL REPORT

Patient: Trissy Jane Beers

The patient has been thoroughly examined and the chocolate cake episode discussed at some length.

Patient freely admits her guilt, but says she doesn't know why she went beserk.

Recommend that patient be put into a funny farm and the key thrown away.

In plain words, she is a nut. A fruitcake.

A loony.

(signed) Dr. U. R. A. Kookoo.

LAST WILL AND TESTAMENT

I, Trissy, being of sound mind and body now write my last will and testament, in case by morning I'm dead.

To Steffi Jones, my ex best friend, I leave my Nancy Drew collection as proof that friendship goes beyond the grave.

To my brother Robert I leave my Monopoly game since he's already stolen all the red hotels.

My brother Mitch probably doesn't want anything I have. I will leave him the two dollars, 43¢ in my elephant bank.

That's it. These are the only people I care about in the whole world, and anybody I left out will realize I left them out on purpose. If people don't care about me, why should I care about them?

I, Trissy

MULTIPLE CHOICE MURDER TEST

(choose one)

Let Daddy's friend "G":

A - Choke on chocolate cake.

B - Drown in a pool of mud.

C - Get locked in a pen with an enraged bull
    when she's wearing a red dress.

Dear Dumb Beers,

Do you remember, Stupid, when you were about 4 years old and you got into Mitch's stamp collection and messed it all up?

In the middle of the night, he crept into your room and woke you up. He said, "I'm going to fix you for messing my stamp collection. I'm taking you to the swamp and I'm leaving you there with all the little slimy biting, crawling, creepy things that will EAT you up and just leave your bare bones!"

I pulled the covers over my head. I was so scared I didn't even dare breath. I stayed under the covers until I almost suffocated. Then I poked out my nose and discovered Mitch was gone. But I hardly slept all night, thinking that any minute he might come back and drag me off to that swamp.

The next day Mom made Mitch admit he was

just threatening me. All he'd wanted to do was scare me into being good. And he did. I never touched his stamp collection again.

When Mom and Dad separated, I thought it was like the swamp--just a threat, a horrible period of time like those suffocating minutes under the covers, and the best thing was not to think about it too much. Then it would be over sooner, and we'd be back to normal.

Was I really so stupid?

Way in the back of my mind, didn't I know better? Didn't I know their separation was for real and for good?

That's the trouble with me, anyway.

I tell myself too many stories.

So, Dumb Beers, do you think you can remember now the way things are?

Are you wide awake this time, Stupid? Open your eyes.

I'm telling you all this for your own good,

Dummy.

Yours in Truth,

I, Trissy

P.S. From now on, stick to the facts.

P.P.S. Just the FACTS, and only the FACTS,

and nothing but the FACTS.

P.P.P.S NO MORE MAKE BELIEVE.

HOW THE FIRE BEGAN

1. I sneaked into Mitch's room and took a book
   of matches, which he is not supposed to
   have, but does, because he is smoking
   secretly. He keeps his matches in his off
   limits desk drawer. (I didn't look at his
   dumb, naked girl books.)

2. I took Nancy Drew collection.

3. I took chewed up stuffed mouse Dad gave
   me during stuffed mouse phase.

4. I took old drawings and stories from third,
   fourth, and fifth grade (which I had been
   saving for when I got famous, to show that
   even as a mere child I had superb talent--ha
   ha)

5. I took china cat Mom gave me during china
   cat phase.

6. I dumped everything into my large plastic
   wastebasket. (My big mistake.)

7. I dropped a lighted match into the basket.
   Drawings and stories went WHOOOSH! into flames.
   Everything else went sputter.

8. I poked up the fire a bit with my back
   scratcher. (Mitch's generous 25¢ Christmas
   gift.)

9. Everything went gooey and soft, and a great
   big cloud of thick, dark grey smoke funneled
   up.

WHAT HAPPENED NEXT

1. I was coughing like mad. The cloud of
   smoke (which stunk like a skunk) was rolling
   toward the door. I tried to shoo it to the
   window. No luck.

2. Loud noises from the hallway. Banging on
   my door. Mom burst in. Uncle Arthur was
   right behind her.

3. Mom shrieked. "Trissy! What are you doing?

My God, the room is on fire!"

4. Uncle Arthur pushed Mom aside and stamped
   on the smoldering, stinking mess of plastic,
   books, and stuffed mouse, getting his shiny
   black buckle boots covered with goo.

5. Mother called me thoughtless, stupid,
   irresponsible, and immature. "Idiot!" She
   grabbed my arm and shook me. "You could
   have set our house on fire, and killed us
   all!"

6. She shook me so hard, my teeth started
   chattering.

7. Uncle Arthur said, "Edith, dear. Please.
   I'm sure she didn't realize...her side of
   the story...thoughtless, but...just a child...
   difficult...adjustment..."

8. Mom began crying. "I don't know, I don't
   know." She put her hands up to her face.

9. Uncle Arthur put his arm around her. "Maybe

you should say something to your mother, Trissy. There must be some explanation. How did it happen? Why did you do it?"

10. I said, "It was like the chocolate fudge frosting on the wall."

11. "Chocolate fudge frosting?" my mother said. She sounded like she was going to start screaming again. "Chocolate fudge frosting! What's the child talking about!"

12. Uncle Arthur said, "Edith."

13. Mom said, "Yes, yes, all right." Her nose was red. "I'll control myself."

HOW I FELT BECAUSE OF WHAT I DID

1. Hard for me to breathe.

2. As if a rock was pressed down on my chest.

3. Stupid and sorry.

4. Dumber than dumb.

5. Tired. Wished I could get into bed, pull the covers over my head, and never come out.

1. "Trissy," my mother said. "Turn around and look at me." She looked so unhappy, I started to bawl. Uncle Arthur's friendly smile got completely unhooked. I was hiccuping and burping. "I'm sorry, I didn't mean to scare you, I didn't want to set our house on fire," I babbled. "I just wanted to get rid of some baby junk, and everything went wrong. Everything always goes wrong."

2. My mother took me in her arms. She held my head against her breast and petted my head. "My poor baby," she said.

3. I was so surprised I stopped crying, hiccuping, and burping. My mother gave a big sigh. "It hasn't been easy for you, has it, Trissy? And now I'm going to tell you something else. I don't know if it will make things better

or worse for you. But you have to know."

4. Uncle Arthur was biting on his pipe. "That's right, tell her everything, Edith. The sooner told, the sooner the adjustment." And then he told me. "Your mother and I are going to be married after your parents' divorce is final." His friendly smile was hooked into place again. "Well, Trissy, how are you going to like having me as a stepfather?"

5. "Sure, that would be okay," I said. My mother and Uncle Arthur looked happy. They didn't ask me, and I didn't tell them, but if it was up to me, I wouldn't choose him for a stepfather, or "G" (whoever she is) for a stepmother.

Dear Father,

I am in quarantine as a punishment. Did Mother tell you what I did this time? Probably.

I want to ask you something. When Mom marries Uncle Arthur, she will be Edith Bronson Beers Jobaggy. What will I be? I mean, who will I be?

Your daughter,

Trissy.

P. S. Did the chocolate fudge frosting clean off okay? I hope so. I'm sorry.

- Hello. Is this Trissy Jane Beers?

- Yes. Who is this, please?

- This is your father, Mitchell Powell Beers.

- Dad! How funny! What a funny way to talk to me.

- Trissy, I want to tell you something very
  serious, actually, and I want you to listen
  to me.

- Okay, Dad.

- Are you still in quarantine, by the way?

- Yes, mostly I am.

- Well, I'm going to speak to your mother about
  that. I think things are going to change,
  don't you? I mean, the way you feel about
  things and act, and--

- I guess so. I mean, I hope so.

- Well, don't cry, honey. We all make mistakes,
  and yours are just childish ones. Now listen
  to me. Here's what I want to tell you. You,

when you were born, were named by your mother
and me. Now you've heard that story enough
times. How much we wanted a girlbaby, and how
happy we were, how very happy. And how I
sat with your mother in the hospital and
called out all sorts of girls' names. Like
'Pamela, come here!' 'Shirley, eat your
oatmeal!' And at last I said, 'Trissy, behave
yourself!' And your mother and I agreed that
was the perfect name for our baby. For you.
And we added Jane because it sounded nice
with Trissy. Fancy and plain, I remember
your mother saying. And then Beers, because
children get their father's last names--
— I know all that, Daddy.
— Sure you do. Well, the point is, honey, you
are Trissy Jane Beers, no matter what your
mother and I do. That's the name you were born
with. That's who you are, and that's what

142

you're always going to be till you get

married someday--

- I know all that, too, Daddy.

- Good. Think about it. When you have trouble,

   it doesn't make you a different person, or

   less of a person, or no person. You are still

   you. Your name is still Trissy Jane Beers.

   It is yours, and whatever that name stands

   for is up to you. Whatever people think of

   when they hear that name depends on you. How

   you act, how you talk, how you dress, what

   you do. Get it?

- Yes.

- It doesn't depend on your mother and me, or

   anyone else, because you are a separate person.

   You are yourself. You are an individual. Do

   you understand, Trissy Jane Beers?

- Yes.

- Good. Don't forget.

- I won't.

FRIENDS RE-UNITED

QUARRELS FORGOTTEN

(Trissy Press International)

May 20. Jefferson City

Trissy J. Beers, and Steffi T.
Jones, both members of the sixth
grade graduating class of Jefferson Elementary School on Spring
Road, today buried the hatchet
and made up their long series
of quarrels.

In separate interviews, both Miss
Jones and Miss Beers told this
reporter they were delighted at
this newest turn of events.

"Actually, it was all so stupid,"
said Miss Jones.

"Well, I'm glad, even though I
also have other best friends

now," said Miss Beers,

referring to Miss Patricia

Crosby who accompanied her

to the interview.

Asked to comment about the

root cause of their vicious

quarrels both Miss Jones and

Miss Beers said, 'No comment.'

Dear Diary,

Mrs. Gilfer says a diary is invaluable. With just a few words to jolt our memories, years from now we can look back and remember so much.

Steffe, Laura, Pat and I ate lunch together today. I had half of Patricia's peanut butter sandwich because I forgot my lunch. Steffi contributed a piece of pound cake (which she despises) and Laura graciously gave me a dill pickle. Still don't like her thrillingly much.

Steffi wrote me a note in Montgomerys's class. "Beers, it was boring these weeks without you."

I wrote her back. "Jones, not for me."

Mrs. Dilfer said I should by all rights be editor of the yearbook, but since the other kids voted for Steffi's creative effort, democracy would have to prevail.

"Still you must help Steffi all you can," she said. She adjusted her false bosoms. "Steffi is so pretty, but prettiness isn't enough, you know. Now THERE'S a good subject for a story, Chrissy."

She is always giving me good subjects for stories. She thinks I want to be a writer when I grow up. But what I really want to be, I decided, is a nurse. Patricia's mother is a nurse, and she wants to be a nurse, and we've agreed to go to nurses' training together. Steffi and Laura

still don't know what
they want to be, which
I think is rather dumb
of them.

More tomorrow.

Yrs. truly, dear Diary,
Trissy Jane Beers